Joseph, Master of Dreams

Kathleen Cook Waldron

For Halee~
Happy reading
and dreaming,

Kathleen Cook Waldron

Joseph, Master of Dreams

Kathleen Cook Waldron

Cover illustration by Carol Biberstein

ROUSSAN
PUBLISHERS INC.
Specializing in YA and fiction for pre-teens

THE CANADA COUNCIL | LE CONSEIL DES ARTS
FOR THE ARTS | DU CANADA
SINCE 1957 | DEPUIS 1957

We acknowledge the support of the Canada Council for the Arts
for our publishing program.

We acknowledge the financial support of the Government of Canada
through the Book Publishing Industry Development Program
for publishing activities.

http://www.roussan.com

National Library of Canada
Bibliothèque nationale du Québec

Canadian Cataloguing in Publication Data

Waldron, Kathleen Cook
Joseph, master of dreams

(Beloved books)
ISBN 1-896184-84-7

1. Joseph (Son of Jacob)--Juvenile fiction. I. Title.
II. Series.
PS8595.A549J68 2000   jC813'.54   C00-900828-4
PZ7.W1466Jo 2000

Cover design by Dan Clark
Cover illustration and interior graphics by Carol Biberstein
Interior design by Jean Shepherd
Typeface Bembo

Published simultaneously in Canada and the United States of America
Printed in Canada

1 2 3 4 5 6 7 8 9 UTP 9 8 7 6 5 4 3 2 1 0

My principal sources for *Joseph, Master of Dreams* include *The Bible* according to the Masoretic text; the Jerusalem and King James Bibles; *Pentateuch and Haftorahs*, Soncino Press, second edition, with Hebrew text, English translation and commentary, edited by Dr. J. H. Hertz; *The Torah: Genesis, A Modern Commentary* by W. Gunther Plaut; *Joseph and his Brothers* by Thomas Mann; and *The Gifts of the Jews* by Thomas Cahill.

I also owe special thanks to the following people for their encouragement and patient guidance with my research, writing, and revisions: Lee Cook, Ann Walsh, Mark and Levi Waldron, Charlene Sachter, Rabbi Paul Laderman, Rabbi Daniel Goldberger, Reverend David Anderson and his family, Marj Penman-Griffin, Jo Bannatyne-Cugnet, and Jane Frydenlund.

For dreamers then and now
and for the man of my dreams
my husband Mark

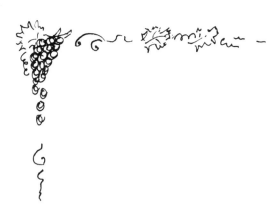

1

Joseph had been walking for days, alone with only the sun and the stars.

"You, there, young man," the owner of a wide field called out as Joseph wandered into view. "What are you looking for?"

Joseph opened his mouth to answer, but his voice failed him. He hadn't said a word since he'd left his father's home in Canaan. This man was the first person he had met.

The older man waited. Joseph cleared his throat. "I'm looking for my ten brothers with our father's flock," he said at last. "They were coming here, to Shechem. Have you seen them?"

"Ten shepherds did pass through here," the man answered. "I heard them say they were on their way to the rich pastures at Dothan, on the trade route from Gilead."

"Dothan," Joseph repeated. He thanked the man and set off at a brisk pace. Daylight lay softly on the field, though the sun was still well below the horizon. If he hurried, he might find his brothers in time for their midday meal.

The farther he walked, however, the hotter the sun burned in the sky. Its heat seemed focussed solely on him. When he could walk no more, he slid his arms out of his rainbow-coloured coat, folded it carefully, and sat down.

I'm close now, he thought, taking a long drink of the water he carried in his bag. *After a short rest, I should find them: sheep, goats, brothers—the whole herd.*

Joseph closed his eyes, stretched out on the warm ground, breathed in the sweet scent of the grassland, and let his mind wander. *When Mother died after Benjamin was born, I thought Papa was going to keep me home with him forever. I can see why he keeps Benjamin home. He's still a child. But I'm seventeen years old. Seventeen! Old enough to go where I please and do what I want.*

Joseph laced his fingers to cushion his head, while his thoughts continued to drift. *I'm glad that when Papa let me go with my brothers the first time, I told him how they sat and chatted and ate while his herd wandered off and was nearly lost.*

Joseph could remember the scene clearly. *My brothers were furious at me for telling on them. They even called me a spy! But Papa was pleased. And why not? Who else could watch his flock and his sons at the same time? I'm sure that's why he let me go all the way to Shechem this time. It's probably why he made me this special coat, too.*

Joseph ran his fingers over the fine fabric of his coat. Each thread seemed to radiate softness and colour. It was the kind of coat worn by a clan chief. A chief! And not one of his brothers had anything like it.

A light breeze rippled through the tall grass. The grass, bending all in the same direction, reminded Joseph of one of his dreams.

In the dream, eleven bundles of wheat, belonging to his eleven brothers, had bowed down to his bundle. Bowed, like this grass in the wind.

How angry his brothers had been when he told them about that dream!

Looking up at the fiery sky, Joseph recalled a second dream. Just as the bundles of wheat had bowed in the first dream, the sun, moon, and eleven stars had bowed to him in his second dream. This dream, even more than the first, had infuriated his brothers. His father's reaction had been strange, too. First he had scolded him as if the dream weren't really a dream at all, but a story Joseph made up. "What is this dream you have dreamed?" his father had scolded. "Shall I and your mother and your brothers indeed all bow down to you?" And worse than the scolding had been the way his father had fallen silent afterward and simply stared at him.

Why was Papa so upset? When he was a young man, he dreamt he heard God's voice and saw the gateway to heaven—a ladder to the sky with angels of God going up and down. Later he spent an entire night, from dusk to dawn, wrestling with an angel. In the morning he rose with the sun, victorious, yet left to walk with a limp forever. No one ever questioned Papa. Why do they question me?

A few small clouds grazed across the sky. One cloud trailed behind the others. *Like me, following my brothers...My brothers!*

Joseph jumped up, grabbed his coat, and started running.

From the top of a hill he saw sheep and goats grazing near an ancient well below him. Ten shepherds watched over the flock. His brothers. "Hello!" Joseph shouted, waving his coat to get their attention. "It's me, Joseph!" Quickly he pulled on his coat and ran to meet them.

"Here comes Joseph, the master of dreams," Levi grumbled.

"Joseph the dreamer, showing off the coat Father made especially for him," Asher added, imitating Joseph waving his coat.

"Joseph, the first son of Father's favourite wife," Gad sneered, "stealing his affection, as if we didn't matter at all."

"Father's favourite son," muttered Dan.

Judah spat. "You mean Father's favourite SPY!"

Simeon's eyes darkened. "Joseph may dream of us bowing down to him," he said, "but I'd rather starve. Or kill the little pest."

"Squash him," his brothers agreed, "then see what becomes of his dreams."

But Reuben, the eldest, interrupted them. "Stop!" he shouted. "What are you saying? How can you even think of killing your own brother."

"We could say a wild animal ate him," Issachar suggested.

"No!" Reuben insisted, his face burning. "We can't hurt Joseph!"

"Why not?" Simeon asked. "Look how he's hurt

us in Father's eyes. He's made us look foolish and in-competent. I say we kill him."

"Foolishness and incompetence are no excuse for murder." Reuben's eyes darted across the landscape, searching wildly for any alternative to his brothers' hateful plan. In desperation, his vision fixed on a single site. "If Joseph thinks he's so far above us," Reuben told his brothers, "perhaps he simply needs more time to think, to clear his thoughts. In a quiet place—like the bottom of this dry well."

The brothers peered down the well's narrow opening.

"Well, well," Zebulun said, his voice echoing in the emptiness. "This should cool him off."

His brothers agreed.

Confident he could rescue Joseph from the well, Reuben guided the herd to a fresh patch of grass shel-tered by a small rise.

But his nine brothers waited beside the well.

Joseph ran across the grassy plain, his rainbow coat billowing out behind him. When he reached his brothers, his cheeks were burning and sweat glistened on his forehead.

"I knew I'd find you today," he said, smiling broadly. He held out his arms to greet his brothers, but instead of greeting him, they surrounded him and tore off his coat.

"Give that back!" he cried.

"Never!" His brothers laughed as Joseph chased his coat from one to another. One of them grabbed Joseph's sack of supplies and flung it out of his reach.

"Thieves!" Joseph yelled. "What did I ever do to you?"

"Spy!" his brothers yelled back.

"I am not a spy!" Joseph shouted.

"Liar!" his brothers shouted back. Joseph made a final lunge for his coat, but his brothers threw it aside and pushed him into the well.

Joseph landed with a thud, raising a thick cloud of dust in the single shaft of sunlight. A silvery snake slithered away. A scorpion skittered into a crack.

"Get me out of here!" Joseph demanded, his voice ambushing him from all sides.

Nine faces stared down at him.

"Look," said Naphtali, "one of Father's lambs has fallen down the well. Hear him bleat?"

"That's no lamb," Simeon laughed, "it's a toad. Hear him croak?"

The brothers moved to a cooler, quieter place for their midday meal. Shaded by a small clump of scrubby trees, they opened their sacks and began to eat their bread. With their backs to Joseph and the well, they saw on the horizon a caravan approaching from the East. Ishmaelites carrying spices, balms, and perfumes to Egypt.

"Leaving Joseph to die *would* be cruel," Judah said slowly. "Why have our brother's blood on our hands when we could sell him instead?"

"Sell Joseph?" asked Issachar.

"Sell . . . our *brother?*" Asher stumbled on the words.

"Joseph, our brother, a slave?" Joseph's brothers chewed on the words as they finished their bread.

"HELP! HELP!" Joseph shouted until his throat was raw, and he felt as if he might drown in his own voice. Still no one came.

His brothers were too far away to hear, but a small band of Midianite merchants coming from the west did hear Joseph's cries. While his brothers finished their meal, the Midianites threw Joseph a rope and fished him out of the pit.

"A thousand thanks," Joseph told them. But his rescuers weren't looking for thanks. Swift as dust devils rising from the sand, they swept Joseph away.

As if they had overheard his brothers' plan, they

took him directly to the Ishmaelite caravan. Strong, healthy young men made valuable slaves. This one was sure to bring a good price.

euben led the herd in a wide circle back
toward the well. "Joseph has been down there long
enough," he told the nearest goat. "Long enough for
my brothers to have had their fun. Long enough for
him to have had some time to think. Perhaps even
long enough for him to have come to his senses and
forgotten his silly dreams."

Reuben approached the well, calling Joseph's
name. When no reply came, he called louder. "Joseph! JOSEPH!" he shouted. When he reached the
well, he leaned so far over the edge that he nearly fell
in himself.

The well was empty.

Reuben ran to his brothers, "Joseph's gone," he cried. "Disappeared!"

The brothers ran back to the well. They looked deep inside, but all they saw was darkness.

"The child is gone," Reuben repeated. "Gone. Joseph, our brother, is no more...Where will I go now?"

In a voice barely above a whisper Levi asked, "What will we tell Father?"

At first no one spoke. Only a dry breeze broke the stillness. Then all the brothers spoke at once.

"We need a plan."

"Yes, a plan."

"A goat! We could kill a goat."

"A goat?"

"Yes, and smear its blood on Joseph's coat."

"Blood?"

"Yes, then we can find a stranger to take the coat to Father."

"He can say he found it."

"And ask if the coat belongs to his son."

"Yes. Yes. A goat. The coat. What else can we do?"

When Jacob their father saw Joseph's coat, he recognized it at once.

"My son's coat. The coat I made him," Jacob's voice was drier than dust. "A wild beast has eaten my son. Joseph is torn, torn apart!"

Jacob ripped his own tunic and dressed in sackcloth. His sons and daughters tried to comfort him, but he refused to be comforted. "Even in my grave will I continue to mourn for Joseph," he told them.

The sun, moon, and all the stars in Jacob's sky turned dark, and only cold sorrow shone in their place.

oseph stood with his head bowed, swaying slightly, trying to follow the discussion of his selling price to the Ishmaelites. His head felt light, not only from the sun and his fall in the well, but also from the speed at which his life was changing.

As the bargaining heated up, Joseph noticed a man filling a water jug from a spring near the animals. How he longed for a cool drink! His tongue felt like a dry leaf rattling in his parched mouth. A thick layer of dust from the well covered him from head to toe. How refreshing a splash of water would feel on his skin!

Moving so slowly that he appeared to be standing still, Joseph edged his way over to the spring. No one seemed to notice him. All their attention was focussed on the bartering. At the spring, Joseph dropped to his knees, cupped his hands, and drew a mouthful of water to his lips. He drank deeply, splashing water all over his face and hands.

His sudden fall caught the eye of a young billy goat. The goat lowered his head and charged. Racing toward his target with precision and power, the goat butted Joseph squarely in the backside and sent him sprawling.

Joseph landed with a splash, face down in the mud, the wind knocked out of him. The goat frolicked around him, unwittingly striking a donkey with his hoof. The donkey brayed. A second donkey brayed back. Then another. And another. The chorus of braying donkeys set off the sheep, which in turn set off the cows, until not a single word could be heard above the racket. A pair of goats ambled over to Joseph and began to nibble on his tunic.

Negotiations stopped. A cluster of slaves hustled over to calm the animals. Joseph sat up, dazed, his face covered with mud.

His new masters wasted no more time bartering. They settled on the standard price for a young slave.

Twenty pieces of silver.

Deep purples and reds were seeping into the sky. With the day's business concluded, the Ishmaelite leaders decided to wait for morning to continue on their way. Attention shifted from Joseph to the work that had to be done to set up tents and prepare meals. Joseph returned to the spring to wash up.

"You, there! Mudhead!" called one of the servants.

It took awhile for Joseph to realize the man was talking to him. "Me?" he asked.

"Yes, you."

"My name isn't Mudhead," Joseph started to explain. "It's..."

"Look, no one cares what your name is. Whatever it is, Mudhead is what you are. Look at you."

The other servants laughed.

Joseph opened his mouth to argue, but his words evaporated on the warm evening air. *Why tell them my name anyway*, he thought. *He's right; no one cares. My old life is gone. My home, my father, my brothers, our flocks, everything. Even my name.*

"Listen, Mudhead, don't just stand there rooted like a tree, get busy and help us put up this tent. Take that corner and tie it over there. Hurry. Our masters are hungry and tired."

Joseph was pulled into a whirlwind of activity.

After putting up the tents, he was ordered to help prepare the evening meal.

At home he had been the favourite child of the master of the house. Most of his time had been spent at his father's side, learning to read, write, and keep track of the family's accounts. His meals had always been prepared for him. He had no idea what to do.

"Mudhead, you lazy daydreamer, get to work. Shell these almonds and pistachios for the masters," ordered a servant.

"Can't they shell their own? At home we always..."

"No one cares what you did at home. You're here now with a pile of nuts to shell. Now get busy and keep quiet."

A small servant boy carrying two bowls stepped up beside Joseph. "I'll help you," he offered. And together they started shelling.

No sooner did they fill one bowl than it was swept away and replaced with another.

"Enough shelling, you two. The fire is burning low. Go gather more dung. Quickly."

"Follow me," the boy said, "but watch out for the goats."

"I will," Joseph assured him.

Following the boy, Joseph noticed he walked with

a limp. "Did you hurt your foot?" Joseph asked.

"I was born like this," the boy told him, "that's why I'm called Twisted Foot."

"Is that what your mother named you?" Joseph's voice couldn't hide his surprise.

The boy laughed. "My mother, like all mothers, saw only my perfections. She called me Mizzah. But now she's gone, and everyone calls me Twisted Foot."

"What do you want *me* to call you?"

"Twisted Foot, of course. It suits me."

Stepping gingerly around the animals, Joseph and Twisted Foot gathered enough dung to fill their baskets. Returning with their full baskets seemed no less risky than filling them had been. Men and women practically ran over each other, rushing back and forth, balancing pitchers, platters, cups, and plates. Some carried fresh food and drink to their masters. Others carted off their garbage.

Not only did the masters have to be looked after, but all the animals had to be tended to as well. Each cow, ox, sheep, and goat had to be fed, watered, and bedded down. Many had to be milked.

In spite of his encounter with the billy goat, Joseph felt more at ease with these animals than he had felt all day. His father's flock had seemed tamer and easier to handle than these creatures. Yet his experience with them gave him at least a small measure of comfort. He didn't have to be reminded to take care in handling them.

Once the masters' bellies were full and they were deeply involved in serious matters, Joseph and Twisted Foot sat down with the other servants to their own meagre meal of thin stew and dry bread. They ate in silence, too tired to speak, grateful for the quiet, for their simple food, and for a brief rest. Joseph could not remember ever feeling hungrier. How long had it been since his last meal? It felt like years.

After the day's final duties were tended to, Joseph lay down on the ground to sleep with the other servants. The others fell quickly into an exhausted sleep. Twisted Foot seemed to lapse into dreams even before he was fully lying down. But Joseph's eyes would not close.

Just as he had done last night when he was still seeking his brothers, he found a smooth stone and placed it under his head. He stared up at the moonless, star-filled sky. Gusts of wind seemed to scatter the occasional sighs, rustlings, and snores of his fellow servants.

But these night sounds could not lull him to sleep, nor did the hard ground keep him awake. He had slept many nights under the stars while searching for his brothers. What kept him awake tonight was something different.

Last night he was travelling through familiar territory. He had the comfort of the fine coat his father had made him. He carried his own food and supplies. He knew he would soon see his brothers. And he knew he would return home.

Tonight nothing was familiar. His coat was gone, he had to depend on strangers for his every need, and he had no idea where he was going or what would happen next.

While everyone is asleep, I could escape, Joseph thought. *I could run away. Find my way back home. Father and Benjamin would be happy to see me. They must be worried, fearing I am hurt or lost or perhaps even dead!*

But what about my older brothers? Did they not throw me down a pit and leave me to die? If I were to return now, would they try to finish me off?

Tangled thoughts churned round and round. But as the new moon rose, a new thought entered Joseph's head, a thought so unexpected it crowded out all the others.

True, I am a slave, a servant to strangers. I cannot imagine where I am going or what will happen to me when I get there. No one here knows who I am or what I did before today. No one cares. All this is true. Yet, for the first time in my life, in many ways I am free. Free from my older brothers' jealousy. Free from Papa's constant supervision. Free to begin my life as a man. Free!

The days and nights passed quickly in a blur of endless work and brief sleep. Twisted Foot clung to Joseph's side, leading him through the days' activities, showing him what to do, and what not to do. Joseph learned quickly, remembering the lessons his father had taught him, remembering to focus all of his attention on the task at hand. Now, not only could he shell nuts and haul dung, he could do a hundred other tasks as well.

Day after day the landscape they crossed resembled the fertile areas that Joseph had always known. New places laced with familiar sights: rolling hills, grassy flatlands, fields of grain crisscrossed with irrigation canals, swaying date palms, almond and olive groves. Then one day their caravan crested a hill. Joseph stopped so abruptly he nearly fell over.

Ponds. Puddles. Rivers. Wells. All these were familiar to Joseph, but never had he imagined water like this. Vast. Open. As far as he could see, rolling blue water and airy blue sky tossed slivers of sunlight back and forth between them. Was the sun shining down from the sky or was its light rising, in thousands of fiery flashes, from the water below?

"What is it?" Twisted Foot asked. "Is something wrong?"

"Look!" Joseph lifted his hand to point, though his eyes made the gesture unnecessary.

"What?" Twisted Foot asked. "That? The water?"

Joseph's voice was barely a whisper. "Yes, the water."

Twisted Foot rolled his eyes. "That's the sea. Haven't you ever seen the sea before?"

"Never," Joseph answered. "Never," he repeated, trying to take in as much sunlight, sky, and water as his eyes would allow.

Twisted Foot glanced at the water, then back at his friend. "The sea's the same as the desert," he told him, "only wetter. Filled with water instead of sand. It will follow us now all the way to Egypt, so you can gawk as you walk." He tugged at Joseph's sleeve. "Come on now. Hurry!" he urged, "We have to catch up. Our masters have no time for sightseers."

As the caravan neared Egypt, an argument broke out between two of the leaders. "Look here, a rat has eaten through one of our grain sacks," one man announced.

"So what?" a second man replied. "How much can one rat eat?"

"But the sack is half empty," the first argued.

"How do you know it was full in the first place?"

"How do you know it wasn't?"

"And I ask you again, how much can one rat eat?"

"How do you know it was just one rat?"

"What is the problem here?" the eldest of the leaders interrupted. The two men tried to explain.

"Our inventory at the end of a journey is never what it was when we began," the elder said. "Some goods we consume along the way, like oil and spices. Others we pick up, like Mudhead."

"True," the first man answered, "but shouldn't we keep closer track of what we actually have?"

"I don't see the point," the second argued, "as long as we have enough to sell and trade at the end of our journey, who cares? Besides, what poor donkey would want to record every item?"

All three men laughed till their bellies ached.

Joseph, working nearby, had overheard every word. Eager for any chance to lessen the tedium of his days, he approached the men cautiously, bowed, and spoke directly to the ground. "If you'll forgive me," he said.

"Forgive you? For what? What do you dare speak

to us about?" the man who cared not about rats asked.

"I can record your items," Joseph offered in a quiet, even voice.

"What?" asked the man who had found the hole in the sack, his face flushed. "You, a servant, think you can tell us how to run our business?"

"Let him speak," the elder said. "I could use a good laugh. Imagine a servant's idea of doing business. Let's hear it."

"If you'll forgive my saying," Joseph repeated, "before I came here I used to help my father keep our family's accounts."

"Is that so?" the rat man interrupted. "Family accounts, you say? And what exactly did you do, Mudhead? Count out pomegranate seeds, so no one had more to eat than anyone else?"

Finding this unbearably funny, the men laughed loud and long. Other leaders wandered over, curious to discover the cause of the commotion. All were talking and laughing as they came. But the elder silenced them.

"Go on," the elder said, "tell us more, but do get to the point."

"Have you any papyrus, sir?" Joseph asked.

"Papyrus?" the elder repeated.

"You planning to build us a boat?" one of the

leaders interrupted.

"And float our accounts down the Nile?" the rat man added, beginning to laugh. One look from the elder stopped him. All eyes then focussed on Joseph.

"Yes, sir, papyrus, Joseph continued. "It is both useful and portable for keeping records."

"What kind of primitive beetles do you think we are? We know the uses for papyrus. We carry all the most up-to-date items, including papyrus. Now what is your point?"

"If you would set a few rolls aside, I would happily weigh, measure, and record all of your goods for you," Joseph said.

"How do we know you won't cheat us or steal from us?" the elder asked.

"I invite you to watch my every move. I promise I'll not take a single seed nor drop of oil for myself. My only wish is to be of service."

Even as he spoke, Joseph knew these words were not entirely true. The promise never to cheat or steal was genuine. But in his heart, he wished for more than simply to be of service to the Ishmaelites. A task as complex as recording all their trade goods should be worth more to them than ordinary slave work. Perhaps twenty pieces of silver? Perhaps enough to earn his freedom by the time they reached Egypt.

"We will think about your offer," the elder told him. "Now get back to work."

Many urgent matters had to be dealt with, so the leaders considered Joseph's proposal only briefly. Being shrewd traders, they concluded, "As long as we watch the servant carefully, and he doesn't neglect his other duties, what have we got to lose?"

The next day Joseph set to work recording all the Ishmaelites' trade goods. With great care, he weighed, measured, organized, and recorded every item.

As the days passed, the leaders watched him with growing interest.

"He is a clever boy," remarked one.

"Quite clever," agreed another.

"He learns quickly."

"Yes."

"He should fetch a good price for us in Egypt."

"Quite a good price," his friend agreed.

4

Egypt shimmered like a lake in the desert. Buildings rose like towering cliffs. Joseph stared at the crowds of people and the stalls piled high with exotic foods, wine, pottery, spices, and fine fabrics of all colours. Strange sights, sounds, and smells beckoned him from all sides. Even the air felt different.

A parting of the crowd drew his attention. There, passing amongst them, was what appeared at first glance to be a large donkey cart. As it drew nearer, however, Joseph could see it was something much grander. A horse-drawn chariot! He had heard of such things, but until now he had believed they were merely the fanciful creations of storytellers.

He hardly knew where to look first. The chariot, beautifully decorated with ornate designs, turned on finely crafted wheels. The slender driver wore elegant, costly-looking garments. But it was the horse that captured Joseph's full attention. Lively, high-spirited, long-legged, and silky black. He had seen one or two horses before at sheep-shearing festivities, but never had he seen an animal with the sleek grace of this creature.

"Look! Over there!" Twisted Foot tugged at Joseph's arm, turning him away from the magnificent chariot and pointing him toward a nearby stall displaying ripe, sweet-smelling fruits. Several fruits were cut, inviting customers to taste their juicy flesh. "What do you say we fill our mouths?" Twisted Foot asked. But before they could get close enough to the fruit to try it, the Ishmaelites hustled them away.

"You have served us well, young man," the Ishmaelite elder told Joseph when they stopped at a noisy central area. "And your cleverness will be rewarded."

I'm being set free! Free! I did it. I earned my freedom. A smile spread across Joseph's face and happiness raced through his veins.

The elder smiled back. "Not only will you fetch a

good price for us on the block, but you will go to a fine household, spared from the endless, back-breaking drudgery of ordinary slave work. No making bricks or moving stone blocks for you. You'll be a high-class slave on a high-class estate."

Joseph's throat tightened. "But, but I told you before, I am not a slave," he stammered, trying to fight back his panic. "I was never a slave. I was kidnapped by the men who sold me to you. Please, please understand. I do not wish to be sold again."

"Silence! There is nothing here to explain and no one who wishes to listen. Remember who you are, young man, and remember your place."

Joseph was herded toward the centre of the slave block. Twisted Foot followed.

"Perhaps we will be sold together," Joseph called to his friend. "Life as a slave would not be so bitter if we were to serve side by side."

Twisted Foot laughed. He could see the hurt in his friend's face, but still he could not hold back his laughter. "I would like that too, my friend, but it is impossible."

"Impossible?"

"Surely you have noticed my size and my foot. Your fine form and cleverness will fetch a good price. But me? My only value is with the men I now serve.

Who would be such a fool as to buy the likes of me?"

"You are a bargain at any price," Joseph called to his friend, but his words were lost as he was pulled up onto the slave block.

Masses of unfamiliar words swirled around him as he was turned this way and that, poked and prodded. Though the words ran together like raindrops in a flood, Joseph understood clearly that he had been sold. He was hauled off the block and shoved toward Potiphar, the captain of the king's palace guard.

"I won't see you again," Twisted Foot shouted as Joseph disappeared into the crowd, "but I will always remember you."

"Farewell, my friend," Joseph shouted back. How easily he and Twisted Foot had become friends. How quickly now they parted.

5

Once again Joseph was forced to begin a new life. Once again he began at the bottom. Though he came to Potiphar's house as a high-priced servant, he was a servant nonetheless. And all new servants had to prove their worth. Joseph was no exception.

Potiphar's household did offer a wider range of responsibilities than the Ishmaelites had. Here he started out not simply as a nut sheller and dung collector, but the duties of latrine cleaner and pack animal were added as well. No job, it seemed, was too dirty or heavy for him.

Unfamiliar with Egyptian words, gestures made his

tasks clear. *Empty these slop buckets over there. Move these oil jars into that cellar. Dig a hole this deep. Clean up that mess.*

One morning as he was going about his work, he paused to savour the sweet scent of almond blossoms floating on the morning air.

From the day he arrived in Egypt, he'd been keenly aware of its smells. Some were sharp and unpleasant, like the stinking piles of fish guts he was ordered to dispose of. Others were more pleasing, like the honeyed scents of baking drifting from the kitchen ovens. The perfumes and incense from distant lands were oddly foreign. Only a few odours reminded him of home, like the almond blossoms today.

"Bring me dat 'peer," a child's voice called, jarring him back to reality. Joseph quickly lifted one of the feed sacks from the pile he was supposed to be moving to a storage room.

"Bring me dat 'peer NOW," the voice repeated. Bent over from the weight of the heavy sack across his shoulders, Joseph raised his eyes to meet those of a small boy standing in his path. He had no idea what the child wanted. He shook his head and tried to continue on his way. Each time he took a step, however, the boy followed him and blocked his way.

Joseph heaved the sack back onto the ground. "My

'peer," the boy repeated, pointing to the branches of a tall bush, "my 'peer."

Tangled in the top branches of the bush, Joseph saw a slender willow. He reached in and pulled it out. The end was sharpened to a point. "Peer," he told the boy as he handed the stick over to him.

"Now f'row it," he told Joseph, "like dis." And he heaved the stick.

As the boy ran to retrieve his toy, Joseph repeated his words *Bring me dat 'peer. Now f'row it, like dis. Bring me dat 'peer. Now f'row it, like dis.* Squatting to lift the sack back onto his shoulders, he heard a voice behind him ask, "Learning baby talk?"

Joseph twisted around. A copper-skinned maid-servant, about ten or eleven years old, stood behind him, laughing. Joseph's face reddened.

"Baby talk?" he asked.

The boy returned with the stick. "Now you f'row it," he said, waving the stick in front of Joseph.

"Now—you—throw—it," the handmaid repeated, "like—this." She went through the motions of throwing without letting go. "Like this," she repeated once more, handing the stick to Joseph.

Joseph stepped into an open area. "Like this?" he repeated, tossing the willow almost out of sight. The boy ran to retrieve it, but the handmaid stayed.

"Yes," she laughed, "like that."

Thus began Joseph's lessons. The handmaid, who was called Tuia, would say when she stepped outside and saw Joseph, "I open the door. The door is open." He would then repeat her words as he went about his work. Each time they passed, she gave him new words to practice, always making sure he understood exactly what he was saying.

The small spear thrower, Joseph discovered, was Dungi, one of Potiphar's sons. At first he was too busy to notice the boy, but Dungi never failed to notice him. Dungi always had a big greeting and a friendly wave for Joseph. And whenever he could, he trotted after Joseph as he worked, chatting merrily. Though Joseph couldn't answer him back, he was beginning to understand more and more of what the boy was saying.

Running here and running there, from before dawn to long after dark, inside the house and out in the fields, Joseph still found time for Tuia's lessons and Dungi's games.

Some days he and Dungi sang silly songs. Other days he steadied the arrow and guided the boy's small arm as he pulled back on the string of his tiny bow.

"How you today?" Dungi called to Joseph one morning.

"Fine as frog's hair," Joseph answered back, "And how's my little Benjamin?"

Only the boy's puzzled expression made Joseph realize what he had said. Dungi was so much like his own little brother that for an instant he had thought he was back in his father's home.

Dungi spoke so often of his friend the slave that Potiphar had his son point him out. Potiphar then watched Joseph closely, noticing how everything the young man touched seemed to thrive, as if his hand were guided by God.

One day Potiphar called Joseph to his quarters.

"I see you work hard, young man," he told Joseph.

Joseph bowed his head and said, "Thank you, master. I do what I can."

"You do the work of three men, yet you always seem to have a moment for my son."

"He's like my own little brother," Joseph answered.

"You speak our language well for a Hebrew," Potiphar continued. "Can you also write?"

"In my own language yes, but not yet in yours."

"Pity," Potiphar sighed.

"I do figures very well, though," Joseph offered, "and I believe figures work much the same way in both our languages." Joseph knew he shouldn't be too forward with the master of the house, but at the same time he recognized an opportunity when he saw one.

"Is that a fact?" Potiphar studied him closely.

"There is no sheet I cannot balance," Joseph answered proudly. His eagerness to escape the back-breaking tasks that filled his days encouraged perhaps a slight exaggeration of his claim.

"How is it a slave can balance figures?" Potiphar asked.

"I was not always a slave, sir," Joseph began. "I...."

"Never mind. I do not really care how or why you learned. I am a busy man. All I need to know is if you are capable of doing the work."

"If given a chance, I can do whatever you wish."

"Hmmm..." Joseph stood perfectly still, waiting, while Potiphar sat stroking his chin. The young slave had to be tested before he could be trusted with any real responsibility. But how could he test him?

"My wife," Potiphar said at last, "likes pretty things. She spends her days pampering herself, and rarely do I deny her wishes. She may have what she wants. That is of no concern to me. But as the head of this household, it is my duty to keep track of all that comes in as well as all that goes out. Including my wife's whimsies. What do her beauty potions and baubles cost me? Watch her expenditures for a month and then report back to me."

"I would be honoured to help," Joseph said simply.

For a moment both men stood as still as figures carved in a frieze. Then Potiphar spoke, "What did you say you were called, young man?"

Joseph was being asked his name! For months he had simply been called *You*. "*You*, bring me this. *You*, do that." Only Twisted Foot, Tuia and Dungi had called him *Friend*. What name did he want Potiphar to call him? Certainly not Mudhead.

"My name is Joseph, master."

"Joseph," Potiphar repeated, handing him the supplies he needed to begin his work, "you may go now."

Joseph accepted the supplies, but still he could not move. Hearing his own name spoken out loud, brought thoughts of his father and his family flooding over him. Tears welled up in his eyes.

"Is there a problem with what I've asked you to do?" Potiphar asked.

"Not at all, master," Joseph answered, struggling for control of himself. "Thank you for giving me this opportunity."

"Don't disappoint me," Potiphar warned.

6

oseph was introduced to a large woman with an ample bosom, smelling strongly of perfume, Potiphar's wife. "This young man," she was told, "has been ordered by the master to make sure all your needs are met."

Potiphar's wife smiled broadly, revealing large teeth. "Very well," she said to the servant who introduced them. Then, barely above a whisper, she repeated, "Very, very well."

For a full month Joseph spent all his days keeping track of her demands. With great care, he recorded every purchase. Fresh milk, with none of the cream removed, for her beauty baths. The finest cottons and linens for her garments. Amethysts, garnets, jasper, onyx, lapis, copper, and gold for her jewellery. Scented oils for her hair. Goose fat laced with cinnamon, juniper, or frankincense to massage into her skin. The list grew longer each day.

As busy as Joseph was, Tuia still gave him lessons whenever they both had a moment. And he often hurried through his midday meal so he could slip outside to play a quick game with Dungi.

At the end of the month Joseph showed his work to Potiphar. His master was impressed not only by the length of the list, but also by its accuracy and attention to detail.

"Imagine that," Potiphar sighed, "three pieces of silver to buy the kohl to shadow her eyes. No wonder my wife is so lovely. She spends more on her face in a month than I spend on my entire body all year.

"You've done well. Now I'd like you try some more serious accounting."

Potiphar watched Joseph carefully. Clearly God *was* with this young man and caused all he touched to prosper.

Potiphar hired a tutor to teach Joseph the fine points of reading and writing his new language.

Joseph had learned all that Tuia could teach him, but he never forgot her kindness. Now whenever they met, they exchanged smiles and pleasantries instead of lessons in vocabulary.

As the weeks passed, Potiphar continued to give Joseph more and more responsibility. Within months Joseph was the sole person in charge of Potiphar's entire estate and all that he owned.

"My home and fields are truly blessed because of you," he liked to tell Joseph. "Everything I have I leave in your hands. The only responsibility I keep for myself is choosing my meals."

As busy as Joseph was managing Potiphar's business, he found himself lying awake one night in his private room, thinking about his family.

Potiphar has shown me great kindness. He depends on me. I cannot abandon him. Yet, there are times I dream of my family. More than twenty years of my life have passed, and I have not seen them since I was seventeen. The years of a man's life are not like stars in the sky or grains of sand in the desert; they are finite and numbered, enclosed in his skin like seeds ripening in a pomegranate. How many more years will Father have till his life is full and complete? Will I ever see him again? And Benjamin? Surely he too has grown from the child I remember. I could send them a message. But what message would I send? That I am a servant?

Father would rejoice to know I am alive. But he would see me as a mere servant, like any other, rather than one with my responsibilities. Would he then want me to return home and live with him? Would I end up spending my days as before, tied to his side? Would my older brothers still envy me? Still wish me gone?

These thoughts kept Joseph awake deep into the night.

7

Long after Joseph had moved on to other tasks, Potiphar's wife maintained a special interest in him. While he had managed her accounts she had grown fond of him, the slender young man with the gentle manner, fine features, strong shoulders, and smooth skin.

"JOO-SEPH! JOOOOO-SEPH!" she called day and night, sending servants to fetch him, like a bucket of water from the well. In addition to his other duties, Joseph had to do all of her bidding, no matter how trivial it was.

"Joseph, bring me some sweets from the kitchen,"

she would demand, when any one of her maids could have brought them as well.

"Joseph, there's a chip in this pitcher. Replace it at once." And Joseph did as he was told.

Each time Joseph completed one of these errands, she would invite him to join her in her chamber. And each time Joseph refused.

Finally, one day he had to say to her, "Look, with me here, my master never has to worry about anything in his house. All that he owns he has placed in my hands. He holds no more authority in this house than I do. He has withheld nothing from me. Except you, since you are his wife. That is how it is, and that is how it should be. What kind of man would I be to change that?"

But Potiphar's wife was used to having what she wanted. Ignoring Joseph's plea, she continued to call for him and try to coax him into her chamber. Always without success.

One feast day Joseph entered the house as usual to begin his work, but found no one there. Potiphar's wife had dismissed everyone for the day. Everyone but him.

He had taken no more than a few steps inside the quiet house when a voice called, "JOO-SEPH! OOOOH, JOOOOO-SEPH!"

He followed the voice to Potiphar's wife's chamber. "How may I help you?" he asked, stopping in the doorway.

Fluttering her eyelashes, she smiled coyly. Joseph did not react, but stood waiting formally at the door.

She continued to stand there, smiling, fluttering, and waggling her hips.

"I have a great deal of work to do," Joseph told her, bowing politely. "Call me if you need something."

The words had barely escaped his mouth, when Potiphar's wife flung open her arms and rushed toward him. For a moment, Joseph stood frozen in cold panic as his wild-eyed mistress drew nearer. Then he ran.

She chased him from room to room throughout the house calling, "Joseph, Joseph dearest!" She chased him until at last she had him cornered. Panting and sweating, she lunged at him and grabbed his robe. Joseph pulled free and ran outside. He kept running, without looking back. But his robe remained in her hands.

When the other servants returned, Potiphar's wife showed them the robe and cried, "Oh, help me! Save me from this disgrace!" she sobbed. "While everyone was away that Hebrew, the one my husband brought here to mock us, chased me through the house. Running and running after me, chasing me, like a leopard starving for a lamb. He chased me until…until he had me cornered."

She stopped and buried her face in her hands. Sobs wracked her body. She wailed and moaned. Her fingertips tore at her scalp while the heels of her hands dug into her eyes. She was the perfect picture of agony. When at last she raised her head again, her eyes were wide and smudged.

Shivering, she finished her story, "He flung off his robe and grabbed me. Ooooh! I screamed and screamed. I screamed so loud he finally ran away. But see here, the coward fled without his robe."

Seemingly exhausted, she dismissed the servants. But she held onto Joseph's robe until Potiphar came home.

Having already told her tale to the servants, she was fully prepared to repeat it to her husband. "That Hebrew servant you brought here," she began, "he…he came to mock me while you were gone." She went on to recount every detail of the incident, just as she had described it to the servants, complete with sobs and shivers.

When she finished, Potiphar immediately had Joseph removed from his home. Custom would have permitted him to have Joseph killed, but even in his anger, Potiphar was keenly aware of his wife's charm. Joseph wasn't the first man to find her irresistible.

Instead of a death sentence, Potiphar chose to have Joseph arrested and thrown into Pharoah's prison.

8

*y brothers threw me into a pit and left me to
die. I was sold into slavery, like a slab of meat in the mar-
ket. I thought I had sunk as low as I could sink, but I
never dreamt of this.*

Dressed in rags and drenched in darkness, Joseph
looked around the crowded prison. Men and shadows
milled about aimlessly. Thick clouds of flies buzzed
everywhere. Legions of beetles skittered by. Slime
oozed from the walls. Spiders dropped from the cob-
web-covered ceiling. Lice and fleas crawled across his
skin, nestled in his hair, tunnelled into his pores. Every breath stung his nostrils and nearly made him gag.

A narrow trench in one corner explained much of the horrible smell. Joseph watched a prisoner straddle the trench and squat. When he finished, another followed. A third stood off to the side and urinated.

The arrival of the jailer with several guards drew everyone's attention. Joseph watched the guards carry in a cooking pot and a water jug.

"Soup," the jailer told him, "your only meal of the day."

The guards placed the large pots on the floor and quickly stepped aside. Prisoners swarmed like flies around the food. Each man reached forward, trying to be the first to dip his bowl into the soup pot or his cup into the water jug. Pushing and struggling, they appeared to spill more than they tasted.

Joseph waited while the others fought for their meagre scraps. After they settled down to their meal, he poured the last thin drops of soup into his own bowl and drank the final sip of water left in the jug.

"You'll have to be quicker than that at helping yourself," the jailer warned him, "or you'll starve in here."

"Wise advice," Joseph agreed, "but easier given than taken, I fear."

The jailer shook his head. "Watch out for yourself," he said before he left. "You can be sure no one else will."

Each time their meal arrived, the prisoners reacted the same way. Little changed from one time to the next, except the smell. Now not only did Joseph's nostrils sting from the stink, but his eyes burned all the time as well.

Did the other prisoners no longer notice the filth? Did they no longer care? Perhaps they were simply too worn down to do anything about it. Whatever the answer, Joseph felt an urgent need to try to help while he still had the strength.

"Have you no respect for yourselves?" he asked one day as his fellow prisoners scrabbled for their scraps.

"Respect? In here?" one of them laughed. "That's a good one."

"This is the king's prison, not any ordinary dungeon. We were all once responsible men," Joseph reminded them. "Why do you behave like beasts?"

"Are we not treated like beasts?" another prisoner asked.

"What concern is it of yours anyway?" asked a particularly hairy man hunched down over his knees.

"We make this place worse than it is," Joseph told them. "We suffer more than we need to."

"Nothing could make this place worse than it

already is," one man laughed, "not even a heap of old catfish like us."

"How would you make it better?" someone asked. "With soft cushions and golden goblets?"

"Forget the cushions and goblets," someone else yelled. "A warm blanket would suit me."

"I'd settle for some dancing girls myself," added another prisoner, setting off a chorus of loud guffaws.

"We could act like men instead of animals," Joseph told them.

"In here? Are you joking?"

"We could divide the soup and water evenly, so each man had a fair share."

"Who'd do that and not keep the best for himself?"

"I could," Joseph told them, "and all of you could watch to make sure I did it fairly."

"And how would we know you weren't sneaking extra bites for yourself while you were dividing up our share?"

A quiet man who had been standing over to one side, spoke up. "I was an assistant to the king's butler," he offered, "and as his assistant I became a skilled server of both food and drink. I could serve while you measure."

"Imagine having our meals served by a butler...in prison!" Everyone laughed, but they decided to give the idea a try.

The next time the guards brought their meal, the men crowded around as before. "Remember— ouch!—our meal—oof!—will be served," Joseph tried to tell them between bumps and jabs. When he finally reached the pot, he was almost knocked into it, which would have spoiled not only his plan, but their dinner as well.

As carefully as he could, with so many men press- ing in on him, he divided up the broth, the half- cooked lentils, and the few chewy threads of goat meat, mutton, or old cow in the pot. When the soup was evenly divided, the butler quickly passed around each portion. Joseph poured everyone's water.

"My soup's still warm," one man bragged between slurps.

"Quite the banquet," the man beside him agreed.

Each meal went better than the last. The food was the same, but there was more of it because each time less was spilled. The men no longer had to guzzle their portions. Those who chose to could savour every sip.

Next Joseph convinced the jailer to let the inmates scrub the prison.

"I ain't no washer woman," one prisoner argued. But the supplies were brought and the work was done. Once the walls and floors were cleaned, water was brought for the men to wash as well.

"From now on," one of the guards announced proudly, "we'll bring extra water every month or two so you men can keep yourselves nice and clean."

Washing seemed to loosen the men's tongues. One man began by saying, "A chamber pot or two would go a long way toward improving the air in here."

"Especially if the pots had lids," added another.

"And if they got emptied once in awhile," added a third.

"But not in the soup pot," came a voice from the back.

At this last comment, the guards' faces darkened. But another prisoner quickly picked up the discussion. "How about putting a curtain around the pots," he suggested, "so we could have a little privacy when we used them?"

"And if we got curtains, maybe we could get some blankets too? I haven't had a blanket in years."

"And what about those dancing girls? Haven't seen one of them in years either."

"Enough! More than enough," the jailer ordered. "I'll see what I can do."

All requests seen as reasonable were granted. The line was drawn, however, at dancing girls. Dancing girls were not considered reasonable.

The blankets were the last items to arrive, ratty and torn, but with plenty of wear still in them. A man who was once one of the king's astronomers claimed his blanket, and asked for some sturdy bronze rings too.

The guards brought the rings, curious to see why he wanted them. They watched with interest as the astronomer rigged up a sling using his blanket, the rings, and the torch holders built into the walls. Once his sling was in place, he had two men boost him up into it. He then began carving on the ceiling with a broken shard of pottery.

"We can't see the sky in here," he told everyone who was watching, "but that doesn't mean we won't see the stars. Beginning with the star god Orion, I'll keep carving until this space is filled with stars. When I'm finished, you'll be able to look up and see the full river of stars spilling across our stony sky."

The prison would never be a palace. It would probably never even be entirely free of fleas, flies, and lice, but it was certainly a better place than it was.

Even in the darkness of the prison, the jailer could see God's light shining on Joseph, and he trusted him with looking after all the other prisoners' needs. Though he was only in his twenties, Joseph was the man the others depended on to listen to their complaints, settle their disputes, and help them with all their problems.

Two new prisoners were brought to Joseph: the king's chief butler and his chief baker. "The captain of the guard himself, Potiphar, has assigned these men to your care," the jailer told Joseph, "to watch over them and see that their needs are met. They may have offended the king of Egypt, but they were once officials in the royal household. And they are still friends of Potiphar. Heed them well."

"Of course, sir," Joseph replied.

Their former high positions seemed to bind the two new prisoners together. One was rarely seen without the other. Yet they shared little in common. The butler seldom spoke, while the baker seldom stopped speaking. He made certain that everyone was aware that he personally knew how to bake thirty-eight varieties of fine cakes and no fewer than fifty-seven different kinds of bread. Given the chance, he would recite every recipe from memory.

Months passed slowly and uneventfully, as time does in closed-in places. Then one night both the butler and the baker had strange dreams. The next morning Joseph saw sadness clinging to them like cobwebs.

"What makes you so sad today?" he asked.

"We've had dreams," the butler began.

"But no one here can tell us what they mean," the baker interrupted.

"The meaning of dreams is beyond all men," Joseph told them. "But tell me about these dreams if they are troubling you."

The butler spoke first: "In my dream, a vine with three branches budded, blossomed, and grew clusters of ripe grapes. I carried the king's cup to the vine, squeezed the sweet grapes into it, then gave the juice to the king."

After a brief pause, Joseph told him, "Your dream means that in three days the king will release you from prison and pardon you. You will then serve him as before."

The butler shouted with joy, "How can I ever repay you?" he asked.

"I ask nothing from you for telling you this," Joseph replied, "except that you remember me with kindness when you are free. Mention me to the king, so I too, may be set free. I was stolen from my homeland, sold into slavery, and did nothing to deserve this dungeon."

Before the butler could reply, however, the baker demanded, "Now hear my dream." And without pausing for a breath, he continued, "In my dream I carried three big baskets on my head, all full of fine bread and fancy baking for the king. The top basket held the best baking of all, but a flock of birds came and carried away every crumb."

Joseph's face darkened. "Your dream means that in three days the king will also release you from prison. But he will hang you from a tree where the birds will peck away your flesh."

"Fool," the baker muttered. "It was only a dream. A dream. Nothing more."

Three days later Pharoah celebrated his birthday. A great banquet was planned. Both the butler and the baker were released from prison. And just as Joseph had said, the butler carried Pharoah's cup as before, but the baker was hanged.

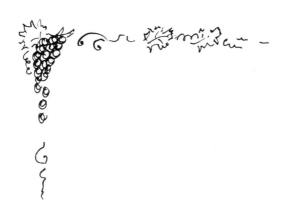

9

The butler had no wish to be reminded of prison. His time there was clouded with memories, like nightmares, that he preferred to forget. Once he was free, he never gave Joseph another thought.

Two full years passed.

Then one night the king dreamt he was standing on the banks of the Nile River. Seven fat cows climbed up out of the water and started grazing on green reeds. Seven scrawny cows followed the fat cows out of the river. These skinny cows, hardly more than skin-covered skeletons, ate the fat cows.

Nothing remained of the fat cows, yet the thin cows were as bony as before.

Pharoah woke up soaked in sweat. But he soon fell back asleep. Again he dreamt.

This time he dreamt that seven full golden ears of grain grew on a single stalk. Seven shrivelled ears then sprouted, blasted by the desert wind from the east, and the seven scorched ears swallowed the seven plump, ripe ears.

Pharoah awoke again. Only moonlight entered his bedchamber. The stalks of grain had been a dream! Still, he lay awake a long time before drifting into a restless sleep.

The next morning Pharoah's spirit was troubled. He sent for all the magicians and wise men in Egypt. In the throne room, he repeated his dreams to these experts.

Some nodded. Others shook their heads. All listened closely to both dreams. But no one could interpret them.

Silence echoed around them. Then the butler spoke. "This day I must call attention to my faults," he said, bowing before the king. "Years ago your servants, the chief baker and I, caused your anger to fall upon us so that we were made wards of the house of the captain of the guard."

"You were sent to prison," the king interrupted. "I remember. Go on."

"One night the baker and I each had a dream, each one our own dream, each with its own meaning. In the prison with us was a young Hebrew who had been a servant to the captain of the guard. When we told him our dreams, he was able to interpret them. And exactly how he said each would be, so it was."

"How was that?" Pharoah asked, leaning forward on his throne.

"I was restored to my royal office, and the baker was hanged."

"So it was! As Pharoah I both know and remember all that goes on in my kingdom. Have this young man brought to me at once."

Joseph was removed from the dungeon with great haste. Out of respect for him, and to honour their king's sensitivities, the guards gave him time to shave and change his clothes before he was led into the throne room.

"I have dreamed a dream, and no one can interpret it for me," Pharoah told him. "I hear you are an interpreter of dreams."

The bright elegance of the throne room after the harsh darkness of the dungeon left Joseph barely able to see, much less speak. But when his words came, they were soft and clear. "Interpreting dreams is not in me, only God can give Pharoah an answer of peace. Dreams, like sunlight on still water, can sometimes reveal what lies below the surface as well as what lies above it. And like sunlight, such dreams are gifts from heaven that no man can capture or hold. If your dreams came from God, then the wisdom to see their meaning may come as well."

"So be it," Pharoah replied. "Now hear my dreams and draw what reflections you can."

Once more Pharoah described his night of dreams. First his dream on the riverbank where the seven fat cows grazed peacefully until seven hideously thin cows came and ate them. After the thin cows finished eating the fat ones, they were still as bony and ugly as they had been before.

"This strange dream woke me up," Pharoah explained, "but later I dreamt again. This time seven silky, ripe ears of grain grew on a single stalk. Seven withered ears, blasted by the east wind, then sprung up and swallowed the seven good ears.

"I have told these dreams to all my best magicians, but not one of them could see their meaning," Pharoah concluded.

Joseph drew a deep breath. "Your dreams are really one dream," he said. "A dream of what is about to happen. The seven fat cattle, like the seven full ears of grain, are seven good years where the land will bloom and produce abundant crops."

"Good, good," the king stroked his imperial goatee and nodded his approval.

"The seven lean cattle, like the seven dry ears of grain, are also seven years. Seven years of famine."

"Go on..." the king prompted, his fingers now twisted in his finely groomed beard.

"Throughout the land of Egypt there will be seven years of fruitful harvests with more than enough food for everyone. After those seven healthy years, however, the land will be consumed by seven years of famine. Nothing will grow. The hunger will be so severe that all the good years will be forgotten. And because this same dream was dreamt twice, it will very soon come to be."

"What can be done?" the king asked.

"During the good years, one fifth of all crops must be set aside or else, during the dry years, people will starve. In the cities, all the royal granaries must be filled with grain."

"Of course," Pharoah interrupted, "that grain could feed many people."

"The king must find a wise and capable man to place in charge of all the food in Egypt," Joseph continued. "And he must also appoint overseers across the land to help collect and store these crops."

"An excellent plan," the king said, smiling at his wise men and magicians. "Now, how can we find a man capable of carrying out such a plan?"

The king's advisers glanced at each other. Some smiled. Others puffed out their chests. But before any of them could volunteer their services, the king spoke directly to Joseph: "Since God's plan has been revealed to you, who could be wiser or more capable than you? From this day forward, your word shall rule Egypt and all its people. Only in the throne shall I remain greater than you."

Many jaws dropped, but no one dared speak. The king's word was law. The king removed his ring with the royal seal and placed it on the finger of his new viceroy. He also gave Joseph a fine linen robe and a gold collar to wear around his neck.

"Come," he told Joseph, "and ride in my second chariot. I want my people to see their new governor."

Joseph rode through the city in a chariot far more magnificent than the one he had admired so long ago with Twisted Foot. Blacker than a starless night, his horse pranced with a proud gait, perfectly aware of where he had to go and exactly how to get there. The chariot's wheels turned smoothly. For the first time in years the wind cooled Joseph's face. The sun warmed his shoulders.

People bowed as he and the king rode by.

Joseph could have ridden for days, but the king had other plans. "I am Pharoah," he reminded Joseph when they returned to the palace, "but as chief of the entire land of Egypt, no one will lift up a hand or a foot without your knowing about it. For this high position you need a suitable Egyptian name. Zaphenath-paneah."

"Zaphenath-paneah?"

"Food-man of life. Fitting, don't you think? And how old are you, Zaphenath-paneah?"

"Th-thirty," Joseph stammered. His head was spinning. In prison little had changed from one day to the next; now the whole world seemed to be changing at once.

"Have you a wife?"

"A what?" Joseph's stomach churned. "No, no wife, but..."

"It is time you had a wife," the king decided. "And I know just the girl. Asenath, the daughter of one of my priests in the sun city of On. She's a fine girl. You'll love her."

Joseph wasn't sure if the king meant this as a prediction or a command. Either way, the king was right.

As soon as Joseph saw Asenath, he did love her. She was soft as flower petals, warm as a summer morning. And she loved to laugh. Joseph spent as much time with her as he possibly could. But his first duty was to Pharoah.

Joseph spent most of his time travelling all over Egypt, collecting and storing food. For seven years, the grain was as plentiful as the sand of the sea and the stars in the sky.

Then came the famine.

10

No crops grew anywhere. Only in Egypt's storehouses was there a surplus of food. People travelled great distances to buy dried grain from Joseph.

In Canaan, Joseph's father Jacob knew that with each passing day his family's food supply was shrinking. Nothing any of them could do brought them enough to eat. Jacob called together all his sons, daughters, grandchildren, and great-grandchildren.

Reuben, Simeon, Levi, Judah, Dan, Naphtali, Gad, Asher, Issachar, and Zebulun came with their families to hear what their father had to say. The youngest, Benjamin, was already waiting by his father's side.

Jacob, the old patriarch, stood before his family, leaning heavily on his walking stick. As crop after crop had failed, his step had grown slower and more uncertain, his limp more obvious.

Surrounded by his family, Jacob felt a sharp pain slice through him. One son was missing. The son who had been gone for so many years. Joseph. Joseph was gone—gone, but never to be forgotten. A tear splashed down Jacob's cheek.

"I have heard there is food in Egypt," he told his family, "so my sons will have to go there. Only Benjamin will stay with me, for he is still too young to risk such a difficult journey. I will send each of you with enough money to buy grain for your entire household. Now you must go, so we may live and not die."

The journey to Egypt blazed hot and dry. The ground burned their feet and the sun scorched their faces. Many times the brothers had to travel at night, guided by the stars, forced to find shelter from the day's fiery heat.

Only when they reached the great sea was the heat eased by a salty breeze. The sight of so much water, sparkling blue and dancing with sunlight, lightened their hearts and helped to quicken their pace. The sea, together with their fear of the hunger their families would soon face, kept them moving ahead, in spite of the weariness that weighed down their bones.

By the time they arrived in Egypt, they were exhausted and covered with dust. Yet they took no time to rest. Instead, they went directly to the crowded offices of Zaphenath-paneah, of Joseph, to join the people waiting to buy grain.

When the brothers' turn came to meet the viceroy, they bowed low before him, their faces brushing the ground.

Joseph recognized his brothers at once, but he spoke to them as strangers through an interpreter. "Where do you come from?" he asked.

"We have come from Canaan to buy grain," they told him, never dreaming this elegant Egyptian was their own brother.

Joseph stood above his brothers, just as he had in his long-ago dream. "You are spies!" he told them through his interpreter. "Spies from our weak border in the Northeast."

"No sir, we are your servants, come only to buy food. We are all one man's sons, honest men. We are not spies."

"You are spies here to see the weakness of our land."

"We, your servants, are twelve brothers, all sons of the same man in Canaan."

"Twelve? I count only ten."

"The youngest is with our father, and one brother is not."

"Your father is still living?" Joseph asked, as if it were simply a matter of curiosity.

"Oh, yes," the brothers replied. "He is well."

Relief touched every corner of Joseph's soul, but all he said was, "Ten strangers claiming to be twelve brothers? As I said before, it's far more likely you are spies. If you expect me to believe otherwise, one of you must go and bring me your youngest brother while the rest remain here. Or else, as the king lives, all of you are spies."

Joseph waited for his words to be translated, then he had his brothers taken away to prison.

After three days, he went to them. And through his interpreter, he told them, "Because I am a God-fearing man, I will give you a chance to prove you are honest men who deserve to live. Only one brother will remain in prison, while the rest take your rations to your families. But after those rations have been delivered, you must return to me with your youngest brother. Only when I see him, will I believe that what you have told me is true. Only then will I spare your lives."

The brothers began speaking among themselves, not knowing Joseph could understand them. "Remember when our own brother Joseph cried to us for help?"

"And we turned away from him."

"Now we need help, who will come?"

"I told you not to harm the child," Reuben reminded them, "but none of you would listen. This is the revenge for his blood, our punishment for having left him to die."

Joseph's eyes salted with tears, but he turned and brushed them away. Turning back, he said to Simeon, "You will wait in prison. The others are free to go."

What choice did they have? The brothers paid for their grain and prepared to leave.

Joseph ordered his servants to fill the men's sacks with grain and give them food for the journey home. He also ordered each brother's money to be secretly returned.

As the brothers made their way back to Canaan, dust blasted every pore of their skin and erased their every step. When they were nearly home, Issachar opened one of his sacks to feed his donkey. There, sitting right on top, was his bag of money. "Look!" he called to his brothers. "The money I paid the

Egyptians is here...in my sack...all of it!"

Trembling like reeds struck by a gust of wind, they asked one another, "What has God done to us?"

11

Jacob hobbled out to greet his sons. The brothers rushed toward him, bombarding him with details of their experiences in Egypt.

"The lord of the land spoke roughly with us."

"He called us spies."

"We told him we're not spies. We're honest men. Twelve brothers, all of the same father."

"Of course, he counted only ten, so we had to tell him one brother was gone, and our youngest brother was home with you."

"He wouldn't believe a word unless we left one brother with him."

"We had no choice. We had to leave Simeon."

"Then the man said we could take our grain and go our way."

"But he said the only way we could prove we're truly honest men and not spies is to bring Benjamin to him."

"When he sees Benjamin, he'll free Simeon, and let all of us go free."

The more Jacob heard, the harder he shook his head. He followed his sons to the granary, feeling as if he too had just completed an exhausting journey. As soon as the animals were settled, the brothers began opening their sacks.

"What's this?" cried one brother, then another, and another, as each one found his money tucked inside a sack. "This money has to be returned," they all agreed. But they were afraid even to touch it.

For a long moment, no one spoke. Then with great difficulty Jacob said, "You are tearing my children from me. Joseph is gone, Simeon is gone, and now if you return to Egypt, I'll lose Benjamin, too. I cannot bear the loss of another son."

Without stopping to think, Reuben said, "Father, you may kill my own two sons if I take Benjamin to Egypt and don't return with him. Let me take him, and I *will* bring him back to you."

"My youngest son will not go with you," Jacob told him. "His brother is dead. If any harm at all were to come to Benjamin while he was with you, it would drive my grey head down into the grave."

The moon filled up and emptied, like a cup dipping into sand and spilling out stars. The parched earth produced not a single mouthful of food. When the Egyptian grain was nearly gone, Jacob had to gather his sons together once more.

In a voice as dry and lonely as the wind, he told them, "Go again to Egypt and buy us a little food."

Judah spoke, and though his words were harsh, his voice was tender. "The Egyptian warned us that we would not so much as see his face without our youngest brother," he reminded his father. "If you send Benjamin with us, we can buy food, but we cannot go without him."

"How could you do this to me? Why did you tell that man you had another brother?" Jacob scolded.

Judah's brothers tried to explain, "The man asked us directly about ourselves and our family."

"He asked if our father was still alive."

"And if we had another brother."

"We had to answer him."

"How could we possibly have known he would

tell us to bring our brother to him?"

Judah silenced the others by saying, "Father, let the boy go with me. That's the only way any of us, our families and our children, have a chance to live and not starve. With my own life, I promise that if Benjamin goes to Egypt, he will return to you safely. If he does not, I will bear the blame for it forever."

Before his words could create any more discussion, Judah added, "We have already lingered here too long. We should be in Egypt now."

Jacob knew he had to act. "If it must be so," he said, "take the finest remaining fruits of the land we have for a gift to this man. Take a little balm, some spices, pistachio nuts, almonds, and a little date-blossom honey, for it is rare in Egypt. Take double the money you took before. Enough to buy what you need now, plus all the money you found in your sacks, in case it was returned by mistake."

The brothers nodded their agreement.

"Take your brother too," Jacob told them. "And may God show you mercy in that man's eyes, so he will release both Simeon and Benjamin. As for me, if I am to lose my children, I will have to lose them."

The days of their journey burned long and hot. The nights baked. Not a single blade of grass cushioned their steps, nor did a single green leaf shade them.

Travelling with Benjamin was especially slow. His first time away from home, he wanted to soak in every new sight, from the smallest insect to the tallest tree. By the time they reached the sea, they were already several days behind. Still, the moment Benjamin saw the water, he ran headfirst into it.

"Come on," he yelled, laughing and splashing and tasting the salt on his tongue. "Join me!"

Zebulun ran in after him. "How can we resist such enthusiasm!" he shouted.

Soon all ten of them were in the water, whooping and hollering like little boys.

That night, in spite of the salt on their skin, they all slept better than they had for a long time.

When at last they reached Egypt, the brothers went directly to Joseph, just as they had before.

The moment Joseph saw Benjamin, he turned and told his servant, "Take these men to my private residence. Then prepare meat so they may dine with me at noon."

The brothers had no idea what Joseph had said. They only knew they were being turned away before they had a chance to speak. They had brought their youngest brother as they'd been told to do. Why then wouldn't the man see them?

As they followed Joseph's servant, all ten brothers shared the same fear, "This must be because of the money that was hidden in our sacks. It's an excuse to trap us, take our pack animals, and accuse us of being thieves."

At the doorway to Joseph's house, the brothers stopped and tried to explain. "Sir, we bought food here once before, and paid for it. But when we got home, we opened our sacks, and there was our money! We have that money here with us, all of it, plus more to buy the food we need now. We do not know who put our money back in our sacks."

"Peace be to you, and have no fear. Your God and the God of your father must have put that treasure in your sacks. I had your money," the servant told them. "Now wait here."

The brothers waited nervously, while the servant returned with Simeon. "Follow me," the servant directed, leading all eleven of them to a large room. He gave them water to wash up and told them, "Your animals will be watered and fed. And at noon, my master will be here with bread."

The brothers washed their feet and prepared their gifts for Joseph.

At noon, Joseph entered the room. The brothers bowed low to the earth and offered him their gifts.

Through his interpreter, Joseph greeted them, then asked, "Your father, the old man, is he well? Is he still alive?"

"Our father is well," the brothers replied, bowing again, "and still alive."

Joseph looked directly at Benjamin, his own mother's son. "Is this your youngest brother?" he asked. "The one you told me about?"

Benjamin bowed and nodded.

"May life be gracious to you, my son," Joseph said, then he ran from the room.

In his private chamber, tears poured from Joseph's eyes as if a cloud had burst inside him. He wept, sobbing and choking, until all his tears had fallen and dried. Then he washed his face and returned to his brothers.

"Serve the meal," he ordered.

Custom did not permit Egyptians to eat with Hebrews, so Joseph had to sit alone at a table apart from his brothers. However, he placed his brothers at a table facing him in the order of their ages—Reuben at one end and Benjamin at the other.

"How could he know our ages?" the brothers whispered among themselves.

Wine, beer, and huge plates of food were served. The more they ate and drank, the more the brothers began to relax. How long it had been since they'd seen such a feast! Roast meat, lentils, olives, dates, breads, pastries, and cakes of every description.

During the meal Joseph supervised the servants, making sure Benjamin had five times as much to eat and drink as anyone else.

While everyone was busy eating, Joseph called his most trusted servant aside and said, "Fill these men's sacks with food, as much as they can carry, then return each man's money to the mouth of one of his sacks."

"It will be done exactly as you ask," the servant told him.

"And put my goblet, my best silver one, just inside the youngest one's sack, along with all his money."

12

The first grey of morning had barely brightened the sky when the brothers were sent on their way with all their supplies. Shortly after they left the city, Joseph sent his servant after them.

When the servant caught up with them, he repeated the words Joseph had ordered him to say. "Why have you rewarded good with evil?" he asked. "How could you steal my master's finest silver cup after all the kindness he has shown you?"

"What are you saying?" the brothers asked. "We would never do such a thing. We returned the money we found in our sacks last time. All of it. Why would we do that, then turn around and steal silver or gold from your master's house?"

The servant said nothing.

Convinced of their innocence, the brothers continued, "If one of us is guilty, let him die, and the rest of us will be your slaves."

"A fair suggestion," the servant replied. Yet Joseph's orders had been clear. "But only the one who took the cup will become a slave; the rest may go free."

"We have no cup," the brothers assured him. "Look for yourself." Moving swiftly, they lowered their sacks to the ground and opened them.

The servant began his search with Reuben, the eldest. Slowly he worked his way down the line. Simeon, Levi, Judah, Dan, Naphtali, Gad. Each man's money lay in his sack, just as before, but no one had the goblet.

Asher, Issachar, Zebulun. The brothers were certain they'd be proven innocent of stealing the goblet. Until Benjamin opened his sack.

There lay Joseph's silver cup nestled in a bed of grain. Its polished surface gleaming in the morning sunlight.

"Impossible!" the brothers cried.

"Come with me," the servant told Benjamin.

"Now."

The brothers tore their clothes in grief, but all of them agreed, "Benjamin will not go alone."

Eleven brothers loaded their donkeys and followed the servant back to the city.

Joseph was still at home. When the brothers saw him, they threw themselves on the ground in front of him.

"What have you done?" Joseph asked. "Didn't you know I would find out?"

"What can we say to you, sir?" Judah said. "How can we argue? Our crime has been uncovered. Now all of us will be your slaves, not just the one found with the cup."

"Far be it from me to do that," Joseph told him. "Only the one with the cup will be my slave. The rest may go home in peace to your father."

Judah took a step forward. "Please sir," he pleaded, "do not let your anger burn against a poor servant like me for daring to speak to a man like you with the power of a king. But there is something you must hear."

Words rose in Judah like water in a spring, flowing clear and pure from a deep, dark place. "You asked us if we had a father or a brother. We told you our father was old, and our youngest brother was the child of his old age. We told you the little one's brother was dead, leaving only him from his mother for our father to love."

Judah paused for a moment, then went on, "When you said you wanted us to bring him here so you could see him, we told you our father would die without him. Still, you insisted we bring him. And our father had to send him to save his family from starving. Now you must know exactly why we cannot leave him."

Judah told him about their lost brother, the one who had been their father's favourite. The brother their father believed had been torn to pieces by wild beasts.

"Since losing him, Benjamin has been Father's only comfort. If we go home without him, sorrow will pull our father into his grave. Please," Judah pleaded, "spare my father and take me instead. I promised my father my life for Benjamin's. Take me and let the boy go home."

Tears flooded Joseph's eyes. He sent his interpreter and all his servants away.

"I am Joseph," he told them in their own language. "Does my father yet live? Can it be true that our father who is so old and who has suffered so much can still be alive?"

Hearing their own language and seeing this powerful man cry, left the brothers without words to answer him.

"Come near to me," Joseph coaxed. "I beg you."

The brothers moved closer, their hearts pounding.

"I am Joseph, your brother, whom you left to be sold into Egypt. You have no reason to fear me nor to blame yourselves for my slavery. God sent me here ahead of you so I could save lives."

No one interrupted.

Joseph went on, "For two years famine has plagued the land. For five more years the soil will neither be ploughed nor harvested. God sent me here before you to safeguard your survival and to save you for a great deliverance.

"Go now and tell our father about his son Joseph—Joseph, whom God has made governor of all Egypt. Tell him to come at once with his family and all he has: his children and his children's children, his herds and his flocks. Have him hurry to my side, so I can look after him. So I can look after all of you."

Out of breath and out of words, Joseph reached for Benjamin. They fell into each other's arms. Joseph then embraced each of his older brothers in turn. All twelve brothers then embraced, wept, and began talking at once. The bitter years that had divided them evaporated like fog burnt off by the sun.

News of Joseph and his brothers spread quickly.
When the king heard, he said to Joseph, "Tell your
brothers I will send wagons for their father, their
families, and all of their belongings. What they cannot carry, I will provide for them when they arrive.
Here they may live and graze their animals on the fat
of the land in Goshen."

"After all these years, Father won't believe you are
alive," Benjamin told Joseph.

"When he sees the wagons and hears about the rich
land waiting for him," Joseph answered, "he'll have to
believe. He'll want to see me with his own eyes."

"It's such a long journey for an old man," Benjamin worried.

But nothing could slow Joseph's eagerness to see
his family reunited. "I'll send ten donkeys with bread
and food just for Father," he said. "Enough to refresh
his spirit like an evening rain on a wilted garden."

Thus preparations were made for a final journey to
Canaan. In addition to all their food and supplies,
Joseph gave each of his older brothers a new suit of
clothes. To Benjamin he gave 300 pieces of silver plus
five new suits of clothes.

On the day of their departure, Joseph rode with his brothers to the edge of the city. "No falling out along the way," he advised them as they left.

Then Joseph waited alone, watching, while his brothers' caravan wound its way toward the horizon through pools of heat as blue as water, shimmering in the sun.

Kathleen, her husband Mark, and their two children, Levi and Rosy, spent thirteen years living in the bush in British Columbia. Levi and Rosy were schooled at home until there were enough children in the area to open a one-room school. Now, Kathleen and Mark live on the shores of Horse Lake and teach adult education in town, though Kathleen reserves her mornings for writing.

Joseph, Master of Dreams has been a work in progress since the late eighties. One of the many fascinating aspects of working with the original story was discovering a lesser known interpretation of Joseph's sale into slavery. While thirty-seven hundred years ago, selling Joseph was a real option for his ten jealous brothers to consider, this traditional interpretation presents an alternate possibility to ponder.

Joseph, Master of Dreams is Kathleen's fifth book for children.